Proverbs 18:21 Living Bible

The tongue can bring death or life;

those who love to talk will reap the consequences.

Proverbs 23:7 Amplified Bible

For as he thinks in his heart, so is he [*in behavior—one who manipulates*]. He says to you, "Eat and drink,"

Yet his heart is not with you [*but it is begrudging the cost*].

Proverbs 23:7-8 Living Bible

6-8 Don't associate with evil men; don't long for their favors and gifts. Their kindness is a trick; they want to use you as their pawn. The delicious food they serve will turn sour in your stomach, and you will vomit it and have to take back your words of appreciation for their "kindness."

Preface

Every child has a dream. Some dream of adventure, others of discovery, and many wonder about their purpose in the world. "The Power of Your Thoughts & Words: Growing Up In GOD's Image" is a story designed to nurture these dreams in young boys by showing them the power of faith, character, and GOD's guidance in their lives.

This story follows Santana, a young boy living in the heart of a bustling city, as he learns profound lessons about life from his wise grandfather, PopPop. Through their meaningful conversations, Santana discovers that he is not just another face in the crowd, but a boy made in the image of GOD— holy, strong, and full of potential.

The journey Santana embarks on teaches him about more than just the world around him. He learns about integrity, leadership, creativity, and most importantly, the significance of living a life that honors GOD. Inspired by scriptures and timeless truths, Santana grows into a young man who understands the value of wisdom, the strength of character, and the importance of trusting in GOD's plan for his life.

This book is not just a story—it is a guide for young boys who are beginning to navigate the world. It encourages them to dream big, lead with integrity, and live with purpose. With the guidance of wise mentors, like Santana's PopPop, and the wisdom found in the Word of GOD, every boy can learn that true success comes from following GOD's path and becoming the person He created them to be.

We hope that "The Power of Your Thoughts & Words: Growing Up In GOD's Image" will inspire young readers to seek GOD's wisdom, build strong character, and pursue the greatest goal of all—to hear GOD say, "Well done, my good and faithful son."

Table of Contents

A Message to my Grandson

Dear Santana,

From the moment you were born, I knew you were special. I've watched you grow from a little baby into the strong, thoughtful, and creative young man you are today, and I couldn't be prouder of you. Together, we've shared so many wonderful memories—those walks in the park, our games of catch and football, shooting hoops at the basketball court, and riding bikes around the neighborhood. Every one of those moments was a gift, but what I treasure most is the time we've spent talking about life, faith, and what it means to be a GODly man.

I remember the first time you asked me about life's big questions, sitting there with me on the rooftop, overlooking the city. From then until now, I've seen you grow in wisdom and strength, always eager to learn more about GOD's plan for you. In every conversation we've had, my hope was to teach you not just about the world, but about the things that truly matter—how to live with integrity, how to show respect to others, and how to trust GOD with all your heart.

This book, "The Power of Your Thoughts & Words: Growing Up In GOD's Image," is a reflection of all the lessons we've talked about over the years. It's about how you are made in the image of GOD, how strength comes from your character, and how leadership is about serving others. It's about living GOD's plan for your life and pursuing the greatest goal of all—to live for Him and hear those precious words, "Well done, my good and faithful son."

Remember, Santana, you are holy; your name means "holy" set apart for great things. Keep dreaming, keep trusting in GOD, and know that He has amazing plans for you. No matter where life takes you, I will always be here, cheering you on and praying for you.

With all my love and admiration,
PopPop

Chapter 1: Made in the Image of GOD

Santana lived in the middle of a busy city, surrounded by tall, gleaming buildings that stretched as far as his eyes could see. His home was an apartment on the top floor of one of those buildings.

Santana loved the city—the people, the movement, and the feeling that life was happening all around him.

But what he loved most of all was sitting on the rooftop of his building, away from the noise, where he could think and dream.

Every evening, just before the sun set, Santana

would climb up the fire escape to the rooftop.

There, he felt peaceful and free. The view was

breathtaking. From his special spot, Santana could

see the lights of the city begin to twinkle, one by

one, as the day turned into night.

Sometimes, he would imagine himself doing great

things—helping others, building something

important, or traveling the world. But often,

Santana wondered what GOD's plans were for

him. What would his life look like in the future?

One day, after dinner, Santana's grandfather,

PopPop, climbed up to the rooftop with him.

They sat on the old wooden bench that had been there for as long as Santana could remember.

PopPop was a kind man, always full of wisdom and love, and Santana loved talking to him about everything—especially about GOD. "PopPop," Santana said, looking out over the vast cityscape,

"I wonder sometimes what GOD's plans are for me. Do you think He has big plans?"

PopPop smiled gently, his eyes twinkling with warmth. "Ah, Santana, GOD's plans for you are greater than you can imagine.

But first, let me ask you a question: Do you know what your name means?"

Santana blinked. He had never thought about it before. "No, PopPop. What does it mean?"

"Your name, Santana, means 'holy,'" PopPop explained. "It means you are set apart, made special by GOD. Just like your name says, you are created by GOD to be strong, mighty, and pure. You are holy, my boy, and GOD has set you apart for something special."

Santana's eyes widened as he let PopPop's words sink in. "So, GOD has something big planned for me?" he asked, his voice filled with wonder.

"Yes, indeed," PopPop said, his voice filled with conviction. "In Genesis 1:27, it says, 'So GOD created man in His own image.' You are made in the image of GOD, Santana. That means you are strong, creative, and full of potential. You are not just any boy—you are crafted by GOD's hands, and His power flows through you."

Santana looked down at his hands, trying to imagine what PopPop meant. He thought about the towering buildings all around him and how they were built by men with ideas, strength, and creativity. Could he, too, do something great like that?

"Being made in GOD's image means that you can reflect GOD's love and power in everything you do," PopPop continued. "It means you can create, help others, and show kindness, just as GOD does. It means loving GOD with all your heart and caring for your family and others, just like Jesus taught in Matthew 22:37-39."

Santana thought deeply about PopPop's words. From that day on, every time he sat on the rooftop, he thought about how GOD had made him holy and full of potential. He began to see his hands as tools for good, capable of building, creating, and helping. He whispered a prayer each morning, thanking GOD for making him special. "I can do all things through Christ who strengthens me," Santana would say, remembering Philippians 4:13.

With his heart full of hope, Santana dreamed of the great things GOD had planned for his life. And up on the rooftop, with the city spread out beneath him, he felt at peace, knowing that GOD's plans were bigger than the tallest building and brighter than the city's lights.

Chapter 2: Strong Character and Values

Santana was growing older, and with every year,

he learned more about what it meant to be a strong

person. He understood that being strong wasn't

just about having muscles or being able to run

fast—it was about having a strong heart and mind.

PopPop often talked to Santana about the

importance of character, especially when they sat

together on the rooftop, watching the sunset.

One evening, PopPop spoke softly, but with

seriousness in his voice. "Santana, strength is not

just about what you can do with your hands. True

strength comes from your heart and mind. The

Bible tells us in Proverbs 4:23, 'Guard your heart,

for everything you do flows from it.' This means that your thoughts and actions are important—they must align with the values GOD has placed in you."

Santana was listening intently, but he wasn't sure he understood. "But, PopPop, how do I know the right thing to do?" he asked, as he pondered every word.

PopPop smiled kindly. "Ah, that's where wisdom comes in, my boy. Proverbs 3:5-6 gives us the answer: 'Trust in the Lord with all your heart, and lean not on your own understanding; in all your ways acknowledge Him, and He will make your paths straight.' When you don't know what to do, trust GOD. His wisdom is far greater than ours."

Santana nodded, thinking about the choices he had to make every day—whether to tell the truth, be kind, or help someone in need. He realized that even small decisions mattered. With each choice, he was shaping his character.

Over time, Santana became known for his honesty, kindness, and fairness. He didn't always get it right, but when he made a mistake, he would pray for GOD's forgiveness and wisdom, just like PopPop had taught him. He remembered the verse from James 1:5: "If any of you lacks wisdom, let him ask of GOD, who gives generously to all without reproach." And so, Santana prayed often, asking GOD to help him make wise choices.

Sometimes, making the right choice wasn't easy. There were moments when his friends would tease him for being different, for not going along with the crowd. But Santana knew that his strength came from within, not from trying to fit in. He knew that doing the right thing, even when it was hard, was what made his character strong.

One day, after helping a classmate who had been struggling in school, Santana sat on the rooftop with PopPop. He shared how difficult it had been to stand up for his classmate when others were teasing him. "PopPop, it wasn't easy. I felt alone. But I knew I had to help."

PopPop nodded, pride in his eyes. "That, Santana, is true strength. Proverbs 28:26 says, 'Those who trust in their own minds are fools, but those who walk in wisdom will be delivered.' You trusted GOD and chose to do the right thing. That is what builds strong character."

Santana smiled, feeling proud of himself. He realized that true strength came from living with integrity, no matter the challenges. As the sun set over the city, Santana knew that with GOD's wisdom and guidance, he would continue to grow in character, just as tall and strong as the skyscrapers around him.

Chapter 3: Leadership, Creativity, and Innovation

As Santana grew into his teenage years, he began to dream even bigger. His time spent on the rooftop, looking out over the vast city, filled him with ideas. He didn't want to just follow others— he wanted to lead, to create, and to make a difference in his city. One evening, as he sat with

PopPop

under the stars, Santana shared his thoughts.

"PopPop, I want to be a leader, but I'm not sure

where to start," Santana said, his voice filled with

excitement but also uncertainty.

PopPop nodded thoughtfully, as if he had been expecting Santana to say this. "Leadership isn't about waiting for the perfect moment to start, Santana. It's about setting an example right where you are.

Remember what the Bible says in 1 Timothy 4:12: 'Don't let anyone look down on you because you are young, but set an example for the believers in speech, in conduct, in love, in faith, and in purity.' You can lead right now, even as a young man."

Santana considered PopPop's words carefully. He realized that leadership wasn't about having a big title or being in charge. It was about making a positive impact, helping others, and showing them the right way to live. From that moment, Santana decided to start leading in his own way, even if it seemed small.

He began by organizing small projects in his neighborhood. When the community garden was overgrown and forgotten, Santana gathered his friends and family to clean it up.   He didn't wait

for someone else to do it—he took initiative.

When winter came, and some families struggled to

get enough food, Santana worked with his

neighbors to organize food drives. Little by little,

Santana was becoming a leader, and people began

to notice.

"GOD has given you a spirit of power, love, and self-discipline, Santana," his grandmother reminded him one day, quoting 2 Timothy 1:7. These words stuck with him. Santana realized that his creativity and leadership were gifts from GOD, and he wanted to use them to make his city a better place.

One day, PopPop took Santana on a walk through a part of the city where new businesses were popping up. They passed shops, cafes, and offices. PopPop stopped in front of a small business and said, "Santana, one day, you could be like these people—an entrepreneur, someone who creates something new and valuable."

Santana's eyes lit up. "Really, PopPop? You think I could?"

"Of course, my boy," PopPop said, smiling.

"GOD has given you creativity and innovation. He has placed big dreams in your heart for a reason. If you trust Him and work hard, you can build something that not only helps you but also blesses others."

From that moment on, Santana's dreams grew even bigger. He began planning ways to start his own projects—whether it was creating new ideas for businesses, helping others, or leading community efforts. He knew that leadership wasn't about power but about service, creativity, and the courage to take the first step.

Chapter 4: Living GOD's Plan

One quiet evening, Santana and PopPop were once again sitting on the rooftop, watching the city lights flicker on as the sun disappeared behind the tall buildings. Santana had been thinking a lot about the future lately, wondering what GOD had in store for him. He turned to PopPop and asked, "PopPop, how do I know what GOD's plan is for me? Sometimes I feel like I don't know what I'm supposed to do."

PopPop smiled, his face full of understanding. "Ah, Santana, that's a question many people ask. But remember, GOD has already written your story. In Jeremiah 29:11, it says, 'For I know the plans I have for you,' declares the Lord, 'plans to

prosper you and not to harm you, plans to give you

hope and a future.'

GOD's plan for you is already in place, even if you

can't see it clearly right now."

Santana looked up at the stars, thinking deeply.

"So even when I don't know what to do, GOD

already has a plan?"

"Yes, exactly," PopPop said. "GOD's plans are always for your good, Santana, even when life seems uncertain or difficult. You just have to trust Him. Pray for His guidance, and He will show you the way. Proverbs 3:5-6 tells us to 'trust in the Lord with all your heart and lean not on your own understanding; in all your ways acknowledge Him, and He will make your paths straight.' Even when the road ahead seems unclear, GOD is leading you."

From that day on, Santana started praying every morning, asking GOD to guide him. He learned to trust GOD's plan, even when things didn't go the way he expected. When he faced challenges—like struggling in school or dealing with friendships—

he remembered that GOD was with him, directing his steps.

One day, Santana faced a difficult decision. He had been offered a chance to join a popular group of kids at school, but he knew they didn't always make the best choices. He didn't want to be left out, but he also didn't want to compromise his values.

Santana went up to the rooftop and prayed, asking GOD to guide him. As he sat there, looking out over the city, he felt a sense of peace wash over him. He remembered Jeremiah 29:11 and knew that GOD had better plans for him than to follow the crowd. He decided to stand firm in his beliefs, trusting that GOD's plan for his life was greater than any temporary popularity.

When he shared his decision with PopPop later that evening, PopPop smiled proudly. "Santana, you are learning to walk in GOD's plan. It takes courage, but GOD will always lead you in the right direction."

Santana knew that GOD's plan for him was good, even when it was hard to see. He continued to trust GOD with his future, knowing that as long as he stayed close to Him, his path would be clear.

Chapter 5: The Greatest Goal in Life

Santana had grown a lot since he was a little boy sitting on the rooftop, dreaming about the future. He had learned about strength, character, leadership, and trusting GOD's plan. But one evening, as he and PopPop sat together, watching the sunset over the city, Santana had a new question on his mind.

"PopPop, what's the greatest thing I can do with my life?" Santana asked, turning to his wise grandfather.

PopPop looked at Santana for a moment before answering. "The greatest goal in life, my boy, is to serve GOD with all your heart. It's to live in a way that honors Him and, one day, to hear Him say,

well done my good and faithful son.

Santana had heard those words before, from the

parable of the talents in Matthew 25:21. The

thought of hearing GOD say "Well done" filled his

heart with a sense of purpose. "That's what I want,

PopPop. I want to live for GOD and do what pleases Him."

"That's the best goal you can have, Santana," PopPop said. "In Proverbs 28:26, it says, 'Those who trust in their own minds are fools, but those who walk in wisdom will be delivered.' Living for GOD means trusting His wisdom and not relying on our own understanding. It means putting GOD first in everything you do—whether it's in your work, your relationships, or your dreams."

Santana thought about this deeply. He realized that life's greatest success wasn't about being rich or famous. It was about being faithful to GOD and following His will. Santana wanted to live in a way that honored GOD, not just for a moment, but for his whole life.

PopPop continued, "Remember, Santana, it's not just about the big things in life. Sometimes, the greatest way we can serve GOD is in the small, everyday choices we make—showing kindness, helping others, and living with integrity. When you do those things, you're living out GOD's purpose for your life."

From that moment on, Santana lived with one ultimate goal in mind: to hear GOD say, "Well done, my good and faithful son." Whether he was helping a friend, working on a project, or dreaming about the future, Santana knew that everything he did was for the glory of GOD. And that, he

realized, was the greatest goal he could ever have.

Chapter 6: Jesus, the Perfect Example

One sunny afternoon, Santana sat with PopPop under the big oak tree outside their building. They had just finished reading the Bible together when Santana asked, "PopPop, why did GOD send

Jesus, His Son, to live on earth?"

PopPop leaned back and said, "Ah, Santana, that's an important question. You see, Jesus came to show us how to live. He is the perfect example of GOD's love and wisdom."

"Jesus had wisdom even as a young boy," PopPop continued. "GOD gave Him wisdom and knowledge. He grew in strength and character, just as Luke 2:52 tells us: 'And Jesus increased in wisdom and stature, and in favor with GOD and man.'"

Santana was amazed. "So Jesus lived with wisdom and character just like GOD wants us to?"

"That's right," PopPop said. "Jesus lived with love, joy, peace, patience, kindness, goodness, faithfulness, gentleness, and self-control—what we call the Fruit of the Spirit (Galatians 5:22-23). These are the qualities of strong character."

Santana thought for a moment. "So if I live like Jesus, I can have those qualities too?"

"Yes, my boy," PopPop nodded. "When we follow Jesus and live by the Holy Spirit, GOD helps us grow the Fruit of the Spirit inside of us. It makes us more like Jesus."

Santana smiled. "Thank you, GOD, for the wisdom of Jesus, and for helping me grow the Fruit of the Spirit in my life."

Chapter 7: Speak Life – The Power of the Tongue

Santana and his grandfather, PopPop, were sitting on the rooftop, their favorite spot in the big city. They had been talking about everything from school to the latest neighborhood project Santana had started. Tonight, however, PopPop wanted to teach Santana a lesson that would change how he saw the world.

"Do you know how powerful your words are, Santana?" PopPop asked, his eyes serious yet kind.

Santana paused, thinking. "I know we should be careful with what we say, but are they really that powerful, PopPop?"

PopPop smiled and nodded. "Yes, they are. The Bible tells us in Proverbs 18:21, 'Death and life are in the power of the tongue, and those who love it will eat its fruits.' The words you speak can either build someone up or tear them down. They can bring life or cause harm."

Santana thought back to a time when he had spoken harshly to a friend and how it had led to an argument. He had seen the hurt in his friend's eyes, but he hadn't realized how much damage his words had done.

"You see, Santana," PopPop continued, "Words are like seeds. Once you plant them, they grow, whether they are good or bad. That's why Ephesians 4:29 says, 'Let no corrupting talk come out of your mouths, but only such as is good for building up.' Our words should bring grace to those who hear them."

Santana remembered something his Nana always said: "If you don't have something kind to say, don't say anything at all." He never fully understood why that mattered so much until now. Words could build someone's confidence or destroy their spirit. It was like having the power to make someone's day better or worse with just a few sentences.

PopPop wasn't done yet. "There's a verse in Proverbs 15:1 that I think you should remember. It says, 'A soft answer turns away wrath, but a harsh word stirs up anger.' When you're in a heated moment, your words can either calm the storm or make it worse."

Santana reflected on times when he had said something in anger and instantly regretted it. It was like throwing a match into a dry forest—one small spark, and everything went up in flames. He realized how important it was to think before he spoke.

"But it's not just about avoiding saying bad things, Santana," PopPop added. "It's about intentionally speaking life. In Psalm 141:3, it says, 'Set a guard, O Lord, over my mouth; keep watch over the door of my lips.' We need GOD's help to speak wisely because our words can be so powerful. When we speak words of encouragement, kindness, and truth, we reflect GOD's love."

Santana looked at PopPop and asked, "So, how do I make sure I speak life, PopPop?"

PopPop chuckled softly. "It all starts with what's in your heart, Santana. Jesus said in Matthew 12:36-37 that we will give an account for every careless word we speak. And in Matthew 15:18, He reminds us, 'What comes out of the mouth proceeds from the heart.' If your heart is full of

love, patience, and kindness, your words will

reflect that. So keep your heart focused on GOD."

As they sat together, Santana felt a new sense of

responsibility. He realized that his words weren't

just sounds—they had power. And from that day

on, he made it his goal to speak life, to build others up, and to reflect GOD's love through his words.

Chapter 8: You Are the Living Testimony of Christ in the Earth

Santana had always admired the way PopPop lived. He was kind to everyone, always had a smile, and seemed to carry a peace that made people feel comfortable around him. One day, Santana asked him, "PopPop, why do you always seem so peaceful and kind to others? How do you always know what to do?"

PopPop smiled, setting his newspaper down. "It's not me, Santana. It's Christ in me."

Santana looked puzzled. "Christ in you?"

"Yes," PopPop said. "As Christians, we are called to be living testimonies of Christ. The way we live, the choices we make, and the way we treat others should show the world who Jesus is. In 2 Corinthians 3:3, Paul says that we are letters written by Christ, not with ink, but with the Spirit

of the living GOD, to be read by everyone."

Santana hadn't thought about it like that before.

"So people should see Jesus in me?"

"Exactly," PopPop said, nodding. "Every time you

are kind, patient, or forgiving, you're showing

others what Jesus is like. When you serve others or

help those in need, you are reflecting Christ's

love."

PopPop went on to explain, "In Matthew 5:16,

Jesus said, 'Let your light shine before others, so

that they may see your good works and give glory

to your Father who is in heaven.' Your life is a

light, Santana. You are a living testimony."

Santana thought about that for a while. It seemed like a big responsibility to carry. "What if I mess up, PopPop? What if I don't act like Jesus?"

"We all mess up, Santana," PopPop said gently. "But that's why we rely on GOD's grace. When we make mistakes, we ask for forgiveness and try to do better. Being a testimony doesn't mean being perfect; it means being faithful."

Santana realized that being a Christian wasn't just about going to church or reading the Bible. It was about how he lived every day. He was called to be a reflection of Jesus to the world, through his actions, his choices, and how he treated others. He was a living testimony.

Chapter 9: Only What You Do for Christ Will Last

One day, Santana came home from school feeling

a bit down.

He had been thinking about all the things people

chased after—money, fame, popularity—and how

it seemed like

everyone was focused on becoming successful.

He wanted to talk to PopPop about it.

"PopPop, why does everyone care so much about being rich or famous? Does it really matter?" Santana asked as they walked together through the park.

PopPop stopped and looked at Santana. "The world makes it seem like those things are important, Santana, but none of it really lasts. Only what you do for Christ will last."

Santana furrowed his brow. "What do you mean?"

PopPop smiled and sat down on a nearby bench. "In 1 Corinthians 3:11-14, Paul tells us that whatever we build in this life will be tested. If we build on things like fame, money, or success, it won't last. But if we build our lives on Jesus— through love, service, and faith—what we do will last for eternity."

Santana thought about all the people chasing after success. "So the only thing that really matters is what we do for GOD?"

"That's right," PopPop said. "The Bible says in Matthew 6:19-20, 'Do not lay up for yourselves treasures on earth, where moth and rust destroy, and where thieves break in and steal, but lay up for yourselves treasures in heaven.' The things we do for GOD—helping others, sharing His love, being faithful—those are the things that will last."

As they continued their walk, Santana realized that he didn't need to chase after the things the world told him were important. What mattered most was living a life that honored GOD.

Chapter 10: The Importance of Commitment and Dedication to GOD

As Santana grew older, he began to understand that being a Christian wasn't just about believing—it was about being committed and dedicated to GOD. One evening, as they sat on the rooftop, Santana turned to PopPop with a serious question.

"PopPop, how do I stay committed to GOD? It's easy to get distracted with everything going on."

PopPop smiled, appreciating the depth of Santana's question. "It's not always easy, Santana. But the Bible teaches us that commitment and dedication to GOD are essential for living a life of faith. Joshua 24:15 says,

'Choose this day whom you will serve,' and that's

a choice we have to make every day."

Santana nodded. He had seen friends who had

started strong in their faith but had slowly drifted

away, caught up in other things. "How do I make

sure I don't lose that commitment, PopPop?"

"Well," PopPop began, "It starts with making time for GOD—through prayer, reading the Bible, and surrounding yourself with people who encourage you to follow Him. Proverbs 3:5-6 says, 'Trust in the Lord with all your heart, and do not lean on your own understanding. In all your ways acknowledge Him, and He will make your paths straight.' When you make GOD your priority, He will guide you."

Santana listened closely as PopPop continued, "Dedication means choosing GOD every day, even when it's hard. It means staying faithful, even when the world tries to pull you away. Jesus said in Matthew 6:33, 'Seek first the kingdom of GOD and His righteousness, and all these things will be added to you.' When you put GOD first, everything else falls into place."

Santana felt a deep sense of peace. He knew that staying committed to GOD was a choice he would make daily, and with PopPop's guidance and the strength of GOD's Word, he was ready to live a life of dedication and purpose.

The End

This story guides young boys on a journey of learning about their identity in GOD, the importance of character, the wisdom of Jesus, and living a life filled with the Fruit of the Spirit. Through the mentoring relationship with his grandfather, Santana grows into a person of strong faith, leadership, and purpose, following Jesus' example of wisdom and love.

Made in the USA
Columbia, SC
05 October 2024